KIDS CAN'T STOP READING
THE CHOOSE YOUR
OWN ADVENTURE® STORIES!

"Choose Your Own Adventure is the best thing that has come along since books themselves."
—Alysha Beyer, age 11

"I didn't read much before, but now I read my Choose Your Own Adventure books almost every night."
—Chris Brogan, age 13

"I love the control I have over what happens next."
—Kosta Efstathiou, age 17

"Choose Your Own Adventure books are so much fun to read and collect—I want them all!"
—Brendan Davin, age 11

And teachers like this series, too:
"We have read and reread, worn thin, loved, loaned, bought for others, and donated to school libraries our Choose Your Own Adventure books."

CHOOSE YOUR OWN ADVENTURE®—
AND MAKE READING MORE FUN!

Bantam Books in the Choose Your Own Adventure® series
Ask your bookseller for the books you have missed

MASTER OF MARTIAL ARTS

BY RICHARD BRIGHTFIELD

ILLUSTRATED BY FRANK BOLLE

An Edward Packard Book

BANTAM BOOKS
NEW YORK • TORONTO • LONDON • SYDNEY • AUCKLAND

RL 4, age 10 and up

MASTER OF MARTIAL ARTS

A Bantam Book / August 1992

CHOOSE YOUR OWN ADVENTURE® *is a registered
trademark of Bantam Books, a division of Bantam Doubleday
Dell Publishing Group, Inc. Registered in U.S. Patent and
Trademark Office and elsewhere.*

Original conception of Edward Packard

*Cover art by David Mattingly
Interior illustrations by Frank Bolle*

ISBN 0-553-29296-X

Published simultaneously in the United States and Canada

*Bantam Books are published by Bantam Books, a division of Ban-
tam Doubleday Dell Publishing Group, Inc. Its trademark,
consisting of the words "Bantam Books" and the portrayal of a
rooster, is Registered in U.S. Patent and Trademark Office and in
other countries. Marca Registrada. Bantam Books, 666 Fifth Ave-
nue, New York, New York 10103.*

PRINTED IN THE UNITED STATES OF AMERICA

OPM   0 9 8 7 6 5 4 3 2 1

MASTER OF MARTIAL ARTS

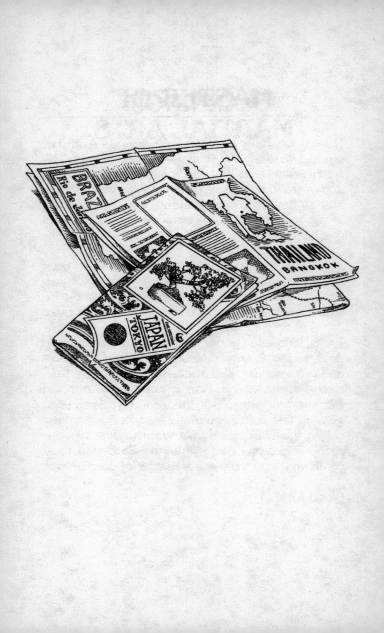

WARNING!!!

Do not read this book straight through from beginning to end. These pages contain many different adventures that you may have as you travel the world in search of your missing friend. From time to time as you read along, you will be asked to make a choice. Your choice may lead to success or disaster!

The adventures you have are the results of your choices. You are responsible because you choose. After you make a decision, follow the instructions to find out what happens to you next.

Think carefully before you make a decision. In your past adventures, *Master of Kung Fu, Master of Tae Kwon Do,* and *Master of Karate,* you traveled through China, Korea, and Japan and had many adventures. But this time you face your greatest test yet as you battle a mysterious enemy called the Dragon. If you want to rescue your friend and come out of this one alive, you must prove that you truly are a master of martial arts.

Good luck!

You are walking to school one morning when Veronica, a fellow member of your high school Karate Club, comes running up to you. "Billy has run off somewhere during the night. His family is very upset. They called me to find out if I knew where he'd gone," she tells you breathlessly.

"I'm sure there's nothing to worry about," you say. "Billy can take care of himself. Especially after everything we went through last summer in Japan." You smile as you think back on all the adventures you and Billy Baxter have had over the years. You remember the first time the two of you went to the Orient to study kung fu. Billy disappeared in China, and you went through all kinds of adventures before you found him.

"I know," Veronica says. "That's just it. His family is afraid that he's on his way to Tokyo—or somewhere—by himself. He left a note saying that he's off to find the 'perfect martial art.'"

"There's only six weeks to final exams," you say. "I wonder what's gotten into him. And why didn't he tell us he was leaving? I mean, we're his best friends."

"He's been acting strange for the past couple of weeks—kind of lost in a daze."

Turn to page 2.

You look at Veronica thoughtfully. "He's all but dropped out of the Karate Club and gone back to concentrating on electronics. He told me he's been working after school on an original computer project. He's taken over his family's garage for his experiments. So why would he suddenly go off in search of the perfect martial art, if there is such a thing? Did the note he left say anything about electronics?"

"No, I don't think so."

"I'd better get over to Billy's house right away," you say.

"I'm going to head for school before I'm late," Veronica says. "Let me know if you find out anything more."

"Okay," you say. You wave good-bye and hurry down the street toward Billy's house.

Go on to the next page.

You don't like being late for school, but it's more important to find out what's happened to Billy. When you reach his house, you see his sister Judy sitting on the steps that lead to the front porch. She waves when she sees you coming.

"Glad you came over," she says. "Mom and Dad are in a frenzy."

"I don't see what all the fuss is about," you say. "Billy's been away before."

Judy nods. "But this time they're afraid that Billy has flipped out—that his mind has snapped from too much studying and everything."

"Oh, come on. Billy is the most down-to-earth guy in school. He knows exactly what he wants to do with his life."

"I always thought so, too," Judy says. "But lately I've been getting worried about him. He's been working all night, every night in his workshop in the garage. He told me he's discovered a new basic principle for building computers. I think he's been working too hard and may have burned himself out."

"But the note didn't say anything about computers or working too hard, did it?" you ask.

Turn to page 64.

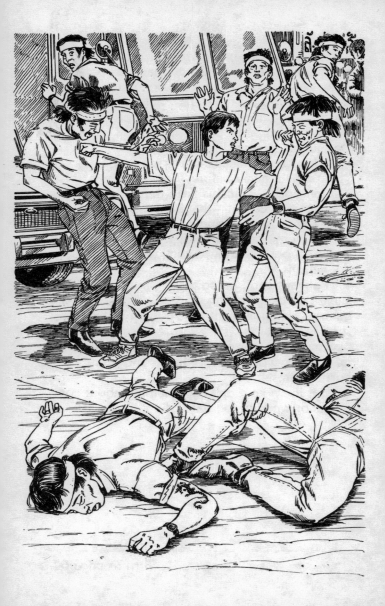

You decide to stand your ground and confront the Thai fighters. You just don't trust the mysterious woman from the plane. At least with the fighters you know what you're getting yourself into. You hold your hands up in a friendly greeting, but the Thais keep charging in your direction. The crowd around you scatters. Police whistles sound from the other end of the block as you swing into action to defend yourself.

Two of the fighters come at you—one from the front and one from the back. You sidestep at the last second and let them crash into each other. Two more are heading at you from the sides. You duck down and lash out with kung fu fists, knocking them both out at the same time.

The fighters who are left run away as the police arrive. You start to explain what happened, but several spectators from the crowd rush over and claim that *you* started the fight. "Don't worry," says one of the police officers, as they drag you off. "You'll like our Thai prisons."

The End

6

Mr. Baxter suddenly notices you standing there.

"Do you know what this is all about?" He looks at you accusingly.

"No," you reply. "I'm as surprised as you are. Can I see the note he left?"

Mr. Baxter strides over and thrusts a slip of paper into your hands. It reads:

Dear Mom and Dad,
   Sorry to leave like this, but I've been called away on an important mission. I must find the most perfect martial art somewhere in the world. I won't be back for a while, but don't worry about me.
                                    Your loving son,
                                              Billy

Billy's mother looks up from her handkerchief. "He didn't even say good-bye. He just packed his suitcase and left in the middle of the night."

"Do you think you can find him for us?" Mr. Baxter asks you. "Don't worry about the expense. I've got enough money saved up."

Turn to page 27.

You think about what Judy has told you as the two of you near the school. "Do you think the man you saw had anything to do with Billy's running off?" you ask her.

"I don't know. If Billy's note had said that he was off to find the perfect *computer,* I'd guess that he'd been hired by this man and asked to keep it confidential. But martial arts? I thought Billy had more or less given that stuff up."

"Well, if you find out anything *else,* call me later," you say. You wave good-bye and hurry to your first class.

You go through the rest of the morning wondering what to do. Billy's family thinks he may be in trouble. If he is, you want to help him any way you can—even if it means dropping everything to search for him. But you can't help thinking that Billy may have had a perfectly good reason for leaving, and that he may return soon on his own. If that's the case, it would be stupid for you to waste your time and Billy's father's money on a wild-goose chase—especially since your final exams are coming up.

If you decide to look for Billy right away, turn to page 41.

If you decide to wait and see if he comes back on his own, turn to page 89.

One of the yakuza guards escorts you to the door of Niko's office and raps in code on the outside door. Niko opens the door himself. He still looks like a bad imitation of a gangster in an American film of the 1930s. He is wearing a broad-shouldered silk suit and a wide-rimmed white felt hat.

"Come in!" he exclaims. "I understand that you are looking for your friend, Billy Baxter."

"You know about that already?" you say.

"Hey, Niko knows everything that goes on around here."

"Do you know where he is?" you ask.

"Of course, but not exactly. He arrived in Japan on JAL flight 276 the night before last. But he never left the airport. He took a connecting flight to Bangkok, Thailand. That's where he is now."

"His sister Judy is also missing," you say.

"I know about that, too. Actually, one of my associates told me about it just before you arrived here. He thinks he knows where they have taken her—anyway, we're working on it."

"They? Who are they?"

Turn to page 30.

You are excited that the porter remembers seeing Billy. At least you know you're on the right track. "Do you know what flight he took?" you ask.

"No, he carried his own suitcase. But I guess he must have taken one of the two early flights. One was a Japan Airlines flight going directly to Tokyo. The other was a Varig flight."

"Varig? What's that?"

"It's a Brazilian airline. Flies straight to Rio de Janeiro. I'd like to get on that flight myself one of these days."

"Thanks for all your help," you say. "Oh, one more thing—did you also happen to see a short, dark-haired Asian or Latino man with high cheekbones?"

"Sure did. Come to think of it, he seemed to be seeing your friend off. I saw them talking over by the ticket counter. After the morning flights took off, I saw him grab a cab out here."

Go on to the next page.

You thank the porter again and head back home. You go over the two possibilities in your mind. Japan seems like a logical place for Billy to head in search of the perfect martial art, and he's been there before. But Brazil? You don't know if they even have martial arts there. Suddenly another thought strikes you—could this martial arts thing just be a smoke screen put up by Billy to mislead everybody about what he's really doing?

If you decide to look for Billy in Japan, turn to page 36.

If you decide to search in Brazil, turn to page 66.

12

You look around at the crowd while you're waiting for the next fight to begin. Suddenly you recognize a woman standing near the entrance. It's the young woman from the plane—you're sure of it! You push through the crowd in her direction but lose sight of her as she ducks into the passageway to the street.

You go out to the street yourself and look around. Suddenly, your martial arts instincts warn you of danger. You turn and spot several figures moving briskly toward you. They all have Thai fighter bands around their heads. Then you notice the woman from the plane standing on the other side of the street. She frantically motions for you to come over. You wonder if she is a friend or an enemy. You have about two seconds to make a decision.

If you decide to follow the woman, turn to page 44.

If you decide to confront the Thai fighters, turn to page 5.

You decide to take the long way around. Ling divides the group into two teams, and when the sun goes down she heads off toward the rope bridge. You start off in the opposite direction with several of the fighters. Somehow you lose the rest of your team in the darkness of the heavily forested mountains. You call out, but you don't hear anything in response except the sound of the wind.

As dawn breaks, you see nothing around you but endless peaks stretching in all directions. You have no idea where you are. All the mountains look the same. You start walking, hoping you're heading back in the direction of your base camp. But after a while, you realize that you have been going around in circles.

It will be a long time before you get back, if you make it back at all.

The End

14

Your father drops you off at the airport early the next morning, and you board the plane for Tokyo a few minutes before its scheduled takeoff. As you walk down the aisle toward your seat, you see that there is a girl sitting in the seat next to yours, looking out the window. You sit down next to her, and as she turns to look at you, you suddenly recognize her as Billy's sister.

"Judy! What are you doing here?" you exclaim.

"I'm going with you," she says.

"Do your parents know about this?"

"Well . . . not exactly," she says.

"Oh great! They're going to flip out completely when they find out that their son and daughter have *both* run off."

"I don't care," she says stubbornly. "I left a long note. They know exactly where I'm going and why."

You slump down in your seat. It's too late to try to change Judy's mind. The plane is already taxiing out to the main runway for takeoff.

Turn to page 84.

Everyone starts up a rocky trail which leads into the mountains. After a while, you reach a cave high above the lake. You follow the others inside. Someone lights a small lantern as Ling hands you a sleeping mat.

"It will be light soon," she says. "We'll rest here for the day and make our move on the Dragon's headquarters tomorrow night."

You lie down, but it takes you a long time to fall asleep. Your head is spinning from all the events of the past few days.

Turn to page 88.

"Can I be of any further service?" the hotel porter asks, setting down your bags in a corner of the spacious sitting room.

"How come you speak English so well?" you ask.

"Most Thais speak English," he says. "It is our second language. We must be very proficient in it before we can graduate from school."

"That's good news for me, since I don't speak any Thai," you say with a smile. "Can you give me a rundown on the sights out there?" You point out the window.

"I'll be glad to," he says. "The broad river you see below is the Chao Phraya, lord of all rivers. The many canals you see stretching out from it are called *klongs,* and as you can see, these are intersected by smaller klongs. And even these branch off into still smaller ones. This extensive canal system is why Bangkok is often called the 'Venice of the East.' Regretfully, many of the klongs are now being filled in to make regular streets. That tall *wat*—or temple, as you call it— rising over there is Wat Arun, the great Temple of Dawn. It is over two hundred feet high."

Turn to page 37.

"I think your son will have to stay out of sight until after the vote in Congress," Martino says. "I'll probably have to wait until he can come out of hiding to interview him."

"I guess I'll go back to my hotel," you say, disappointed. It sounds as if Senhor Barros has more important things to do than teaching you about Capoeira.

"No, you can't do that!" the old man says. "You were followed here by Armada's men. They are waiting for you down on the avenida. They may think you know where my son is."

"How do you know we were followed?" Martino asks.

"A runner of mine, a small boy named Chico, saw you arrive in your car. Seconds later, some of Armada's men pulled up nearby. Then Chico took a shortcut up here to tell me you were coming. Chico, come out here where my new friends can see you."

A small, dark-skinned boy peeks out from behind the old man and smiles broadly.

"What should we do?" you ask.

"Some of my son's supporters have a house about a hundred kilometers up the coast. You can both stay there for a few days, until after the vote," the old man suggests.

If you accept his offer, turn to page 78.

If you decide to go back to your hotel anyway, turn to page 109.

You manage to keep yourself occupied for the rest of the day watching the exotic Thai shoreline go by. Just before sunset, you eat a dinner of rice, fish, bamboo shoots, and watercress with Vajira and the crew. The boat continues on for another few hours after dark. There are no lights along the river, but a rising half-moon silhouettes the tops of the trees along the banks of the river.

Finally, Vajira gives three flashes with her flashlight. These are answered with three flashes from a spot on the dark shoreline up ahead. The boat slows and heads for the shore. A few minutes later, it pulls up to a small pier, dimly visible in the moonlight. Vajira and the crew speak to one another in whispers as you all leave the boat. Your group is met by a man on the pier. You notice a military-type jeep parked nearby.

"We'll drive from here," Vajira whispers in your ear.

You climb in the back of the jeep, and Vajira gets in the front with the driver. The crew of the boat remains behind.

Go on to the next page.

The jeep starts off immediately, bouncing over a dirt road without turning on its lights. You hope the driver knows where he's going—you can barely see your hand in front of your face, let alone the road.

After about an hour of driving, climbing steadily up into a series of steep hills covered with thick vegetation, the jeep comes to a stop at the edge of a small airfield carved out of the jungle. A small, single-engine biplane with pontoons is parked nearby next to a small shack.

Turn to page 58.

"Well, he's sort of connected with the underworld," you explain.

"A gangster?"

"I guess you could call him that. Over here they call them the *yakuza*. But they're not exactly like American gangsters."

You remember Tokyo pretty well from your last trip. When you emerge from the subway you quickly locate the inn.

"This little building is the inn?" Judy asks, sounding skeptical.

"Don't worry, you'll like it."

You ring the bell at the front gate. It opens, and a woman in a kimono bows ceremoniously and greets you in Japanese.

"We would like a room for—" you start in English.

"Ah, so. Follow please," she says, beckoning to you as she starts across the small courtyard.

She leads you inside the main building to a room in the back. It has Western-style beds and dressers on both sides. But the room also has floor-to-ceiling *shoji* screens that when closed divide it into two smaller bedrooms. Each side has a *tokonoma* alcove with a hanging calligraphy scroll and a flower arrangement. The floor is covered with *tatami* mats. You instinctively reach down to take off your shoes.

Turn to page 53.

"Oh, no, you're not going out and leaving me here alone. We're sticking together no matter what," Judy says. "Remember, it's *my* brother we're looking for."

Reluctantly, you agree, and the two of you leave the inn. You find a cab and give the driver the address of Niko's office building.

After a few minutes the driver glances back at you. "Someone following us, I think," he says.

You look out the back window. A large black limousine is two car lengths behind, keeping pace with your cab.

"I try lose them if you want," the driver says.

"Good idea," you say.

The cabdriver speeds up and makes a sharp turn down a side street, blowing his horn. Pedestrians scatter out of the way.

The black car stays right behind your cab. Up ahead, you see a truck backing out of a garage. Your cab narrowly makes it past as the truck continues to back up. You hear the screech of brakes behind as the pursuing car skids to a stop on the other side of the truck.

"That was close," you say, looking out the back of the cab.

But Judy suddenly screams, and you turn around just in time to see your cab run head-on into another car. You feel yourself flying forward over the front seat, then everything goes black.

Turn to page 71.

You decide to go to see Niko first. Groggily, you get to your feet. Your head is still throbbing with pain, but you are determined not to let that stop you. You start to leave, but the police officer says something angrily to you in Japanese.

"Honorable policeman think better you wait for ambulance—take you to hospital for checkup," a bystander says.

"Tell him thanks, but I'm just fine," you say, starting down the street. You turn the corner at the end of the block and, now out of sight of the police officer, start to jog away from the scene.

Every time your foot comes down on the pavement, it feels as if you are being hit on the head again. Fortunately you find another cab a few blocks away and give the driver Niko's address. This time you are not followed. The cab moves slowly through the heavy traffic going toward the center of the city and finally pulls up in front of Niko's tall, glass-sheathed building.

You pay the driver and go inside, where you take the elevator up to the thirty-third floor. When you come out of the elevator and into the corridor, several yakuza guards rush over and quickly search you for weapons. Two of them are missing fingers. You remember from your last trip that this is one of the marks of the yakuza.

Turn to page 9.

"Well, I don't know," you say. "It's only a few weeks to final exams. Billy may be back in a few days with a logical explanation."

"Or he may be off in some distant country again, this time confused and disoriented," Billy's mother says, choking back a sob.

"I'll have to think about it," you say. You go back outside. Judy is still sitting on the front steps.

"I'll walk you to school," she says. "We'd better hurry. We're late already."

The two of you start off down the street.

"Is there anything about Billy's behavior at home that's been unusual lately?" you ask.

Judy looks thoughtful for a moment. "Come to think of it, there is one thing. About a week ago, a strange man came to the house and talked to Billy. Mom and Dad weren't home. I just got a glimpse of him as they went into the garage."

"What did this man look like?"

"Very peculiar somehow. He had straight, very black hair, high cheekbones, and slightly slanted eyes. And he was not very tall."

"An Oriental?"

"Maybe, but he could also have been Mexican or Latin American. I didn't get a very good look at him."

Turn to page 7.

You decide to call Senhor Barros right away. There is a phone on a small desk in the foyer of your hotel suite, and you pick it up and dial the number Maria gave you. It rings a few times, then an answering machine clicks in. A recorded woman's voice comes on and states first in Portuguese and then in English that Senhor Barros is not there but that he can be found at the Garota de Ipanema Café in Ipanema.

That sounds like a strange message for an answering machine, you think. But after all, you are in a foreign country. You go down and ask about the café at the information desk in the lobby of the hotel.

"It is very famous," the woman there tells you. "Garota de Ipanema means 'Girl from Ipanema.' The café was named after a song that was very popular some years ago."

You hail a taxi in front of the hotel, jump in, and give the driver the address of the café. The driver laughs as he maneuvers the cab out into traffic. "That's one address I don't need. I've already been there three times tonight."

"Do you know a Senhor Barros?" you ask.

"Jorge Barros? *Sim, certamente.* Of course," the driver replies.

"I've heard he knows a lot about Capoeira."

Go on to the next page.

"I am sure he does. He is also one of the people fighting to save the Amazon rain forest. The cattle ranchers want to burn it down to make grazing land, and the homesteaders are trying to create farms. Soon all the forest may be turned into desert."

As you are trying to imagine this, the taxi driver pulls over and stops in front of a crowded outdoor café. "Here we are," he says.

Turn to page 73.

"It seems that you have come up against a powerful enemy. He is called the Dragon," Niko says.

"Why would I have an enemy here?" you ask. "I just came to bring back my friend Billy from his strange quest."

"Things are a bit more complicated than that," Niko says, putting his arm around your shoulder. "It seems that your friend has allied himself with the Eagle, one of the richest and most powerful men in the Orient."

"But—" you begin.

"Sit down on the sofa, and I'll try to explain it to you."

You do as Niko says, but you can hardly believe what he is telling you. What has Billy gotten himself mixed up in?

Turn to page 67.

"Martial arts?" Maria asks. "I'm not sure what you mean."

"Like karate or kung fu," you explain. "Have you heard of them?"

"Oh, yes, karate. I know all about it. I see it often on television. It is very popular in my country."

"Are there any martial arts that are found only in Brazil?"

"I know what you mean, like *Capoeira,*" Maria says. "It has a long history in Brazil. It goes back to when the first slaves were brought over from Africa. Many were warriors in their native lands who were captured in battle by other tribes and later sold to the Portuguese slavers."

"Is Capoeira anything like karate?" you ask.

"As a matter of fact, it is very similar in many ways. Originally, the warriors worshiped Ogun, an African god of war or vengeance. His symbol was a dagger stained with blood, and the warriors became great fighters with this weapon. But in the Americas they were usually no match for the hired gunmen of the plantations, who were often armed with pistols and rifles. Later, slaves were forbidden to carry any weapons, so they had to learn to fight empty-handed."

Turn to page 68.

The flight to Bangkok is uneventful. The businessman works for about an hour on his paperwork. You doze off, exhausted by all you've been through in the past two days.

You wake up as the plane is coming in for a landing at Don Muang Airport, twenty miles from Bangkok. As you get out of the plane, you feel as if you're walking into a furnace. The heat is paralyzing. You hope that you'll get used to it. You go through customs and board a bus going to the city. The young woman from the plane is not on it.

As the bus leaves the airport, you look out the window at the rice fields stretching in every direction. The fields are surrounded by ridges of earth that also direct the flow of water in narrow channels between the fields. In the distance, the delicate spires of several Buddhist temples reach skyward.

Once you reach the bus station, you take a cab to the Rama, the hotel where Niko has made a reservation for you. After you check in, you go up on the elevator to your room on one of the upper floors. A porter carries your bags and leads you into an enormous luxury suite. Fortunately, it is air-conditioned. Its large, round windows offer a spectacular view of the city.

Turn to page 17.

"The Eagle and the Dragon have been enemies for many many years," Niko tells you. "Their animosity goes all the way back to their early Hong Kong days when they were direct competitors in the import-export business."

"And now the Dragon wants to foul up the Eagle's plans out of spite," you guess.

"You catch on fast, my friend. The Dragon and the Golden Ear Yakuza also are old enemies. We will do all we can to help you. At the moment I assume you want to go to Bangkok and look for your friend."

"I have to find Judy first," you say.

"I'm afraid that if the Dragon's men have her—and I believe they do—you won't have much luck. You'd better leave that to your friend Niko and the Golden Ear Yakuza. I'll have our people in Bangkok reserve a first-class hotel for you."

If you decide that you must look for Judy first, turn to page 100.

If you decide to go to Bangkok right away as Niko suggests, turn to page 55.

"Hurry, let's get inside," the woman says. "They might get lucky and spot us on deck."

The inside of the cabin has long benches on both sides that double as beds. A table in the center is covered with maps and illuminated by a single kerosene lamp. You can tell that some of the maps are of Thailand and the surrounding countries. Others are unfamiliar and labeled with the strange Thai lettering.

You sit down at the table, and the woman sits down across from you. "What's going on?" you ask her. "It looked like someone was out to get me for some reason."

"Didn't Niko explain all that to you in Tokyo?" she says.

"You're working for Niko?" you ask, surprised.

"No, not exactly. My name is Vajira. I'm working for the Eagle. But Niko and the Eagle are both fighting the Dragon."

"I can't believe the Eagle and the Dragon have nothing better to do with their lives than come after Billy and me," you exclaim.

"Well, I can tell you that the Eagle is a great admirer of yours," Vajira says. "After seeing you in action back there, I must admit that I too am very impressed. But then, I've heard stories about you for some time."

Turn to page 48.

You decide to go to Tokyo and look for Billy. It's not like him to lie, and Japan seems like a more likely place for him to go in search of the perfect martial art. You hurry home to get ready for the trip. When you get to your house, you explain the situation to your mother.

"We'll just have to wait until your father gets home from work to talk about it," she says. "Must you always be running off to these faraway places?"

"This is an emergency, Mom. I have a feeling that Billy is in some kind of trouble." Especially since he's been hanging around with that suspicious-looking man, you think, but you don't say so out loud. You don't want to worry your mother any more than you have to.

That night at the dinner table, you repeat your plans to your father.

"Mr. Baxter called me at the office today," he says. "If you're willing to go after Billy, he will cover all your expenses. I'll go by your school tomorrow and see if we can work something out about the exams."

"Thanks, Dad, that's great," you say.

"I just hope you'll be careful," your mother says.

Turn to page 14.

You thank the porter and give him a tip. After he leaves, you go over and sink down into a large, overstuffed sofa. In front of the sofa is a wide coffee table covered with tourist brochures, many of them printed in English. You pick up one that lists exhibitions of Thai boxing. It is illustrated with photos showing various Thai fighting techniques. The techniques are strikingly similar to those of the tae kwon do you studied in Korea. You begin to see why Billy may have come here to Thailand in search of the perfect martial art. You put the brochure in your pocket to examine more closely later.

After unpacking, you go back down to the street and try to decide where to go first. You could take a look around the city and get your bearings or try to find one of the boxing matches listed in your brochure.

If you decide to look around the city,
turn to page 85.

If you decide to find a boxing match,
turn to page 72.

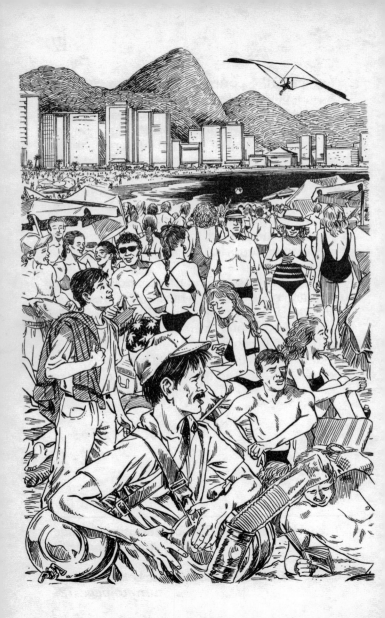

Luckily, you brought your bathing suit. You put it on under your clothes and head down to the lobby and outside. You cross the six-lane Avenida Atlantica and the sidewalks with their mosaic wave patterns. You're amazed at how wide the beach is. You pass a full-sized soccer field and several volleyball courts as well as hundreds of sunbathers, picnickers, and roving bands of amateur musicians before you reach the water.

You leave your clothes in a neat pile on the beach and plunge into the surf. You swim out into the ocean and let a wave carry you back to the shore.

After a few minutes you decide that it's time to get back to your search. Reluctantly, you put your clothes back on over your wet bathing suit and return to the hotel. You take out the telephone number of Maria's friend, Senhor Barros. You wonder whether you should call him now or wait until you look around and get the feel of the city.

If you decide to call Senhor Barros right away, turn to page 28.

If you decide to look around the city first, turn to page 106.

"No, that was just one of his agents," Billy says. "Only a few close associates are ever allowed to see the Eagle, or even to know where he is."

A few weeks later, Billy forms a company that immediately starts building a multimillion-dollar electronics development plant. You begin to wonder if Billy has been corrupted by all that money. But a short time after that, he starts the construction of a huge nonprofit center that will bring people from all over the world to study the philosophy and practice of all the martial arts. He appoints you the director of the center.

The End

You decide that you'd better not wait. If Billy's in trouble, you've got to help him. You hurry home right after school. Your father is still at work, but you explain your plan to your mother. She is worried about your missing school so close to exams, but she agrees that the most important thing is to find Billy.

You decide to try the airport first. If Billy is going to travel around the world in search of the perfect martial art, he will have to fly. As you board a bus for the airport, you wonder how Billy got enough money to travel so extensively. Maybe the man Judy saw is financing Billy's trip.

You get off the bus in front of the overseas terminal. Nearby you see a uniformed porter unloading suitcases from the trunk of a taxicab. On a hunch, you run over and show him Billy's picture.

The man scratches his head as he examines the photograph. "Yeah, I remember this kid. I saw him this morning, very early. I was just coming on my shift."

Turn to page 10.

"This my relief person," the cabdriver says. "Many more drivers in Bangkok than cabs." The second man hops into the cab and drives off.

Your driver leads you through the throng on the sidewalk into a passageway between two two-story buildings. Seconds later, you emerge into a large open-air arena. It's jammed with people, all of whom seem to be in a state of excitement. In the center of the arena, illuminated by spotlights, is a conventional boxing ring. Next to it sit the members of a small orchestra. Several musicians are beating on both ends of tubular drums, others are playing cymbals, and still another is playing a high-pitched, flutelike instrument. The music adds to the noise created by the spectators, and the combination is deafening.

Two fighters, one in blue and silver trunks, the other in bright scarlet trunks, are in their corners, jumping up and down to warm up—not that they need to in the stifling Bangkok heat.

Your driver shouts to a man who is standing on a box nearby, making gestures with his hands. You realize that he is placing and taking bets.

"The next fight will begin in a few minutes—when they sound the gong," the driver shouts to you.

Turn to page 94.

You decide to follow the woman. You dash into the traffic, dodging cars, trucks, three-wheeled taxis, and motorbikes. As you reach the center of the wide, crowded street, you hear a shout and then a thud behind you. You don't have time to look around and see what happened. Two of the Thai fighters are after you. One of them springs at you from behind as another leaps over the hoods of several cars in an effort to cut you off.

Fortunately, you're a master of the martial arts, trained for just this sort of combat. You jump to one side a split second before the first fighter strikes and deliver a flat-handed karate blow to the back of his neck as he flies by. He goes down, unconscious, as a car slams on its brakes to keep from running over him. Then you see the foot of the other attacker coming up, aiming for your head. You deflect his kick with one of your own, stepping inside his attack and delivering a knock-out blow to his chest.

You see two more Thai fighters starting across the street as you reach the other curb. You also notice several Thai police officers hurrying toward you from the other end of the block. The woman is waiting for you beside the entrance to a passageway. You run after her as she disappears into the opening.

Turn to page 51.

A year later Billy finally returns home. Everyone is very happy to see him and relieved that he's all right. His family had just about given up hope.

"It was an opportunity I couldn't pass up," Billy tells you. "I now have enough money to do whatever I want."

"You mean you found the perfect martial art?" you ask.

"Not exactly," he says. "I searched all over the world—in Tibet, Mongolia, Latin America, and Southeast Asia, among other places—but I found that each martial art has its strong points and also its weaknesses. The whole thing was a crazy test designed by this eccentric billionaire, who calls himself the Eagle. The fact that I searched was the important thing to him."

"Was that man who came through town the Eagle?"

Turn to page 40.

At the end of three minutes, the gong sounds to end the round. The fighter in the blue trunks seems to be getting the worst of it. He staggers to his corner where one of his handlers pours a bucket of water over his head.

The gong sounds for the second round, but a few seconds into it, the fighter in the red trunks knocks out his opponent with a tremendous kick to the head. The loser is carried off on a stretcher.

The crowd suddenly quiets down as everyone moves around collecting or paying off their bets.

"Are there any rules?" you ask the driver, who has just come back from settling a few bets. "I see they can hit below the belt without penalty."

"Fighters can hit anywhere—in the stomach, back, throat, legs. But not allowed are biting, hair pulling, or kicking in the head when the opponent is completely down."

"Oh, great!" you say sarcastically.

"Excuse me for moment. I must place some bets on next fight," the driver says, moving back off into the crowd.

Turn to page 12.

"You've heard stories about me? From whom?" you ask Vajira.

"That I can't tell you at the moment, but you will learn soon enough," Vajira tells you. She points to one of the maps on the table. "We are going upriver to Uttaradit. We should arrive there sometime tomorrow evening. This vessel is disguised to look like a river houseboat, but actually, it's quite a speedy launch."

That night, you and Vajira sleep on two of the benches along the cabin wall. Your bench is hard and narrow, but you sink into a deep sleep almost immediately, lulled by the gentle hum of the motor.

When you wake up early the next morning, Vajira is already up and is eating breakfast with one of the crew members. The aroma of freshly brewed coffee hangs in the air.

"I see you are awake," Vajira says as you sit up. "How about a Thai breakfast?"

She hands you a flat wooden plate with some strange-looking food on it. "This is a mixture of ground coconut and fried bananas," she says.

Go on to the next page.

"Mmm, tastes good," you say, eating with your fingers the way Vajira and the crewman are doing. You quickly gulp down the food. You realize that you haven't eaten anything since lunchtime the day before. When you finish, you lean back and look at Vajira. "By the way, I still don't know what this is all about or why we're going upriver."

Turn to page 86.

You hurry through the dark passageway behind the mysterious young woman. When you emerge at the other end, behind the stores that face the street, you find yourself on a narrow path beside one of the klongs. The woman boards a small motorboat a short distance ahead. She starts the outboard motor just as you jump in. The boat roars away into the darkness.

The boat speeds along the canal. The woman steers it masterfully, weaving around the scores of boats moored in the canal that you can barely see in the darkness. Soon the canal intersects with the Chao Phraya. Far across the river, you can see several tall temples rising toward the sky, their gilded surfaces brilliantly illuminated, their reflections shimmering across the water.

The woman steers the boat into the middle of the river. She signals with three short flashes of light from a small flashlight. Her signal is answered from a boat farther out. You can barely see its low-lying, dark silhouette against the light from the other shore. Several minutes later, you pull up alongside a large houseboat, with platform decks at both ends and a long central cabin covered with a curving roof. Two men help you and the woman climb aboard, then one of them jumps into the motorboat and speeds away. When it's some distance away, you see a searchlight strike out from the shore and catch the smaller boat in its beam.

Turn to page 35.

"Paulo says that there is something wrong here," Martino says. "We'd better get back in the van."

But several men with machine guns rush out of the house and surround you before you can make a move.

"I think our boss, Senhor Armada, would like a word with you," one of them says in heavily accented English.

The gunmen force you, Martino, and Paulo into the back of a truck. Two men with machine guns jump in behind you, and the truck starts off.

Ten minutes later, it comes to a stop beside a grass landing strip. A sleek twin-engined Aerostar is parked there with its engines warming up. The gunmen transfer all three of you to the plane, and it takes off immediately.

Hours later, you look out the window and see the twisting course of the Amazon down below. The plane touches down on a landing strip beside the river, and you are all taken aboard a motor launch that is docked nearby.

The boat speeds along the river for the rest of the day and all through the night. For hours, the jungle is burning on both sides of the river. Sometimes the smoke blows across the river, and you can hardly breathe.

Turn to page 90.

"May keep shoes on if wish," the woman says. "We try to accommodate American guests. Must be tired after long flight. Shower and towels in bathroom at end of hall."

The woman bows and leaves the room.

"How does she know that we had a long flight?" Judy asks. "It's almost as if she were expecting us."

"I don't know. I didn't make a reservation or anything. We must be obvious tourists. I guess it's easy to tell that we just flew in from the States."

You and Judy take turns in the bathroom washing up. After that, you use a phone in the hallway to call your friend Niko, boss of the Golden Ear Yakuza.

"May I speak to Niko-san?" you ask.

"Who calls?" a deep voice asks.

You give him your name and wait.

Niko's voice comes on the line. "Ah, my American friend and karate fighter. Welcome back to Japan. We need to talk, but not over phone. You come to my office. You remember address?"

"How could I forget?" you say.

You go back to your room. Judy is staring out the window. "Why don't you stay here and relax while I go and see what I can find out from my friend," you say.

Turn to page 24.

"All right, Niko. I'll let you find Judy, and I'll go to Bangkok and look for Billy," you say.

"Good. I'll have one of my drivers take you to the airport. He'll stop by your hotel on the way and pick up your luggage. And don't worry, we'll keep an eye on you in case one of the Dragon's agents follows you to Thailand."

An hour later, you are at the JAL desk at the airport buying a ticket to Bangkok. Then you sit in the waiting section pretending to read a book. Actually, you are looking around, trying to see if anyone is taking a special interest in you. You notice a young Oriental woman not far away who glances at you from time to time. You can't tell if she's Chinese, Japanese, or neither, but she looks strangely familiar. You wonder if she could be an agent for Niko, or for the Eagle or the Dragon, or if you're just getting paranoid.

Sometime later, you board the plane to Bangkok. The young woman you noticed in the terminal sits a few seats behind you. A respectable-looking Japanese businessman holding a briefcase and dressed in a well-tailored business suit has the seat next to yours. You look for missing fingers and tattoos—another sign of the yakuza—but neither is in evidence, so your seatmate probably isn't one of Niko's men. You settle back for the flight.

Turn to page 32.

"I overheard you say that you are looking for Jorge Barros," Martino continues. "I am looking for him also. I've been assigned to do a story about him. I am quite disturbed that he is not here."

"Maybe he'll show up later," you say.

"Maybe, but somehow I don't think so. I was about to leave the café and go to see if his father knows where he is. His father still lives in the Rocinha favela, which is what you would call one of the slum areas of the city. He refuses to move."

"Where is this place?" you ask.

"Actually, it's not far from here. If you want to come with me, you are welcome. I have a car."

The man looks harmless enough, and with all your martial arts training, you feel you can take care of yourself. On the other hand, you don't want to walk foolishly into danger. Maybe it would be safer for you just to look around the city on your own.

If you go with Martino, turn to page 80.

If you decide to decline and try to see some more of the city, turn to page 106.

"I'd like to go along with you in the plane, Ling," you say.

"Good. Vajira will maintain radio contact with us," Ling says.

You say good-bye to Vajira and climb in next to Ling in the plane. She warms up the engine for a few minutes, then the plane speeds across the small field and takes off, missing the tops of the trees by inches.

The cockpit of the plane is dark except for the bluish light of the instrument panel. In front of you is a small screen. Ling taps it gently with one finger. "This is a position locator," she says. "One of our agents has infiltrated the Dragon's head-quarters. He is carrying a miniature radio trans-mitter that broadcasts on an ultrahigh frequency, one we hope the Dragon doesn't know about. If we can get close enough, a dot of light should appear on this screen to show us where he is."

You and Ling fly for what seems like hours, listening to the steady drone of the plane and the crackling of the radio as Ling keeps in contact with her sister. After a while, the contact is lost.

"That's not a good sign," Ling says. "We should be able to keep radio contact farther than this. I hope everything is all right back there."

Turn to page 93.

A voice comes out of the darkness from the direction of the plane—a voice that you think you remember. You're not sure until the figure is close enough for you to recognize the person talking. It's your friend and kung fu teacher, Ling!

"Ling!" you exclaim. "What are you doing here?"

"I'm here to help you and Billy," she says. "I look after my students no matter where they are." She smiles. "I see you've met my younger sister, Vajira."

"I thought you looked familiar, and now I know why," you say, turning to Vajira. "But you're Thai, and Ling is Chinese."

"We have the same mother, but different fathers," Vajira says. "Sadly, Ling's father was killed in the Cultural Revolution in China, the national tragedy that took so many lives. Our mother fled to Bangkok, where we have many relatives. She remarried here in Thailand, where I was born."

Turn to page 76.

"Now we have to keep an eye out for Shan Hu Lake," Ling says. "Ah, there it is!"

You catch the momentary reflection of moonlight off a lake directly below. Ling circles downward, and with incredible skill brings the plane in for a perfect landing on the water. Then she taxis up to the shore. Seconds later, voices call out of the darkness on the lake bank, and she answers in Chinese.

You climb out of the plane and onto one of the pontoons. In the dim light, you can barely make out a group of figures on the shore, all dressed in black kung fu uniforms. After you and Ling climb up on the bank, she talks to them in Chinese, pointing at you several times. A murmur of approval goes around the group.

"I explained to them that you were one of my students," Ling says. "A student who has since become a master of the martial arts. They are glad to have you along."

Turn to page 16.

The next day you go for another swim and then enjoy a meal at one of the outdoor cafés. The day after that you spend lying on the beach and watching the crowds. This is really the way to live, you think.

As many days go by, you find it more and more difficult to remember why you came to Brazil. Before long, you completely forget that you're supposed to be searching for Billy.

The End

"We want you to go to see Niko," Toku says. "But you wear wire for us when you do. We listen conversation. Maybe find clue to some of his operations."

"I couldn't do that," you say.

"Maybe, maybe not. Remember you are in our country now. Things go badly for you if not cooperate. After all, you want find friends."

If you agree to wear a wire when you see Niko, turn to page 83.

If you refuse, turn to page 101.

Suddenly several helicopters roar overhead and land in a field nearby. As paratroopers storm out of them, the gunmen flee in panic. Armada starts to run, but you quickly bring him to the ground. You don't need any of your martial arts skills, just an old-fashioned football tackle.

An officer from the helicopter hurries over and orders his men to take Armada into custody. "I arrest you in the name of the government," he says. "You went too far when you kidnapped Senhor Barros." You stand up, brush yourself off, and watch as they drag Armada toward the waiting helicopters.

"It was all just a little joke," Armada cries out.

"What's going to happen to you is no joke," the officer says.

You, Martino, Paulo, and Barros are flown to Brasília, the capital of Brazil, as heroes. The next week, your picture is on the cover of *Manchete,* and several lavish parties are thrown in your honor. You appreciate all the attention, but you don't feel quite right about it. Billy is still missing, and you're no closer to finding him than you ever were.

The End

Judy shakes her head. "You'd better go into the house and read the note yourself. Maybe you'll be able to figure it out."

You cross the front porch and enter the living room. Billy's father is pacing up and down. His wife is sitting on the sofa, sobbing into a handkerchief. It takes a moment before they realize that you are in the room.

Turn to page 6.

You decide to look for Billy in Brazil. You rush home and explain your plan to your parents.

The next morning, your father drives you to the airport, where you board a plane to Rio. As the plane takes off, you glance at the magazine the woman next to you is reading. The title is *Manchete,* and it's written in a language you don't recognize. The woman notices your curiosity and smiles.

"My name is Maria. Maria Lins. You are on vacation to Brazil?" she asks you.

"Well . . . not really. How about you?"

"I just had my vacation in your country. It is very beautiful, but I am already *saudade,* homesick for my own. I am a Carioca. That is what we call someone from Rio."

"Is your magazine printed in Brazilian?" you ask her.

Maria laughs. "We speak Portuguese," she says. "People often get our language mixed up with Spanish. It is similar, but there are a lot of differences."

"Do you have any martial arts in your country?" you ask.

Turn to page 31.

After you are seated, Niko goes on, "You must know the reputation that you and Billy have in the Orient. A number of important people have followed your exploits. One of these is the Eagle, a very eccentric billionaire who sends large amounts of money to people all over the world. He admires the fighting skills of both of you very much. The Eagle, through one of his agents in your country, started Billy on a search with the promise to fund his computer research company if he is successful. He feels an outright gift might have seemed, well . . . tacky, as they used to say in the old movies. Also, the Eagle thinks of this as a kind of test."

"Why didn't Billy just tell me all this before he went off?"

"I'm sure that part of the deal was not to tell anyone about it until he accomplished his mission."

"Then how do *you* know all about this?" you ask him.

"I told you Niko knows everything. Actually, one of my associates 'persuaded' one the Eagle's agents to spill the beans, as they used to say. You see, it's all very complicated."

"All right," you say. "But where does the Dragon come in?"

Turn to page 34.

"Empty-handed," you repeat. "That's what karate means in Japanese. It developed originally in China because the Buddhist monks were forbidden to carry arms, so they developed empty-handed techniques to defend themselves. Are there Capoeiras today?"

"Oh, yes. You see, in order to practice their moves under the noses of their captors, the slaves turned Capoeira into a kind of dance. The authorities could never forbid dancing even then. Dance is the soul of Brazil. Today the Capoeira dance is carried on as an art form."

"When I get to Rio, can I find them?"

"Definitely," Maria says. "You will see many demonstrations, though not always with the real experts."

"How can I find the real ones?" you ask.

"I have a good friend in Rio who is an expert on Capoeira. I will give you his telephone number, and also the name and address of a good hotel just across from the beach in the Copacabana section of the city."

Maria writes down the information for you on a slip of paper, then goes back to reading her magazine. You stay glued to the window, catching glimpses of land and ocean far below through breaks in a sea of clouds.

Turn to page 112.

Suddenly, a soft, low whistle, almost indistinguishable from the wind, comes out of the darkness ahead.

"That is my inside agent," Ling says, as a figure appears in front of you.

"Quick! Follow me," the agent says.

You all follow him through a small door at the base of the fortress. Ling's skilled fighters quickly overpower the few guards inside.

"We are lucky. The Dragon was overconfident. He never thought that his isolated headquarters could actually be attacked," Ling says.

The Dragon himself is not at the fortress. But after a few minutes of searching, you find Billy and Judy locked in a dungeon.

"Am I glad to see you!" Billy exclaims as you release him.

"Same here," Judy says.

"You've got a lot of explaining to do," you tell Billy.

"I know, but let's get away from here first. This place gives me the creeps."

The End

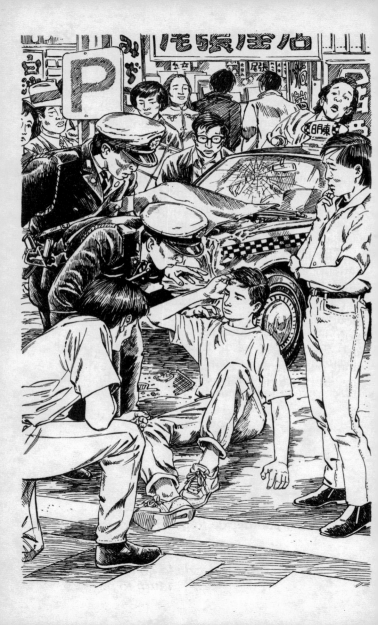

When you come to, you are lying on the ground. Your head feels as if it's been hit with a sledgehammer. Several people, including a police officer, are standing over you. Painfully, you sit up. The officer asks you a question in Japanese which you don't understand.

"I'm all right . . . I think," you say, looking around. The cab you were riding in is parked off to the side, its front end smashed in. There's no sign of the other car—or of Judy. "I was with a girl. Does anyone know where she went?"

"Girl and cabdriver taken by men in other car," one of the onlookers says. "They not seem badly hurt. Men also start take you, but when honorable police arrive, they drive off fast."

Oh, great! you think. First Billy runs off, and now his sister has been abducted. What should you do now? You could go to the authorities and have them check the hospitals, or you could continue on to see Niko and ask him to help you look for both Billy and Judy.

If you decide to go to the authorities,
turn to page 95.

If you decide to go to see Niko,
turn to page 25.

You decide to find one of the boxing matches. You hail one of the small, three-wheeled cabs that crowd the streets in Bangkok. Its wheels are scooter sized and it has a canvas top.

You pull out the brochure from your pocket and give the driver an address on Phet Buri Road.

"You go see boxing match?" the driver asks.

"Yes. Do you know anything about them?"

"But of course. I am big fan. Boxing most popular sport in Thailand. You will enjoy it. We have best fighters in world. May look like just sport but carries on ancient warrior tradition."

The driver takes you to a section ablaze with neon lights. The street is crowded with people from all over the world. Some are wearing Hawaiian shirts, some are in the military uniforms of various countries, others are wearing business suits. Some of the women are dressed in Western-style clothing, while others wear traditional Chinese dresses of embroidered silk.

"Where is the boxing exhibition exactly?" you ask, stepping out of the cab.

"Don't worry, I take you there myself," says the cabdriver, getting out. He waves to someone on the crowded sidewalk. The man runs over and talks to your driver in Thai.

Turn to page 42.

You climb out of the taxi and head toward the café. Luckily, a couple is just leaving a small table at the edge of the sidewalk, and you grab it. You are hungry after your long trip, and you haven't eaten since your arrival in Brazil. Unfortunately, the menu is in Portuguese.

"Can you recommend something?" you ask the waiter when he comes to take your order.

"Our *moqueca* is very good tonight—that's seafood cooked in coconut milk and palm oil."

"Sounds good to me," you say.

While you're waiting for your meal to arrive, you sit and watch the crowd on the street. The people all seem to be enjoying themselves. Many move down the street to the constant samba rhythm you seem to hear almost everywhere you go in Rio.

Turn to page 111.

You munch on some of the seeds while she explains your strategy. "Here's where we are now," she says, pointing at one of the maps. "You can see the lake outlined here. The Dragon's headquarters are over here." She points to another spot. "We determined the exact position last night. Now as I see it, there are two possible routes. Both are probably heavily guarded. The most direct route goes through this pass here and over a mountain chasm. The only way across for miles is a crude bridge, which is actually no more than two heavy ropes strung over the gorge— one rope for the hands and one for the feet. It will be very difficult to cross, particularly at night.

"The other route takes a long way around, avoiding the chasm. It includes some difficult rock climbing, and will take a long time, but it's probably safer than the rope bridge. To make sure that some of us get through, I'm dividing us up into two teams. You can go with either group."

If you decide to take the more direct route across the rope bridge, turn to page 113.

If you decide to take the long way around, turn to page 13.

"Now we work together for the Eagle," Vajira continues. "One of his missions in retirement is to stop the Dragon—the man responsible for a good deal of the drug traffic in the world. In addition, the Dragon finances many international terrorist groups."

"Nice guy!" you say sarcastically.

Ling nods. "I'm afraid that the Dragon has kidnapped your friend Billy and his sister. He has them imprisoned in his headquarters high up in the mountains on the border of Laos and southwestern China, three hundred miles northeast of here."

"We've got to save them!" you exclaim. "What can we do?"

"We will have an assault team heading toward the Dragon's headquarters on the ground," Ling tells you. "We also need an aerial reconnaissance to direct them to their target. Unfortunately, my plane can carry only one passenger. You are welcome to go along, but it would be equally helpful for you to stay here and help maintain radio contact with me and with the ground party."

If you decide to fly with Ling on her reconnaissance mission, turn to page 57.

If you decide to help maintain radio contact, turn to page 114.

You don't know if you were hypnotized by the monk or if you suddenly saw the promise of ultimate truth in his eyes. In any event, you forget all about your search for Billy and spend a year studying in a Thai monastry. You discover the perfect martial art—the pure power of the mind. You know that with total concentration, you can predict every move of an opponent before he or she makes it. You can become an invincible shadow, impossible to strike.

When you finally return to the United States, you find that Billy has returned before you—having searched in vain for the ultimate martial art. He and your family are overjoyed to see you again. You can hardly wait to tell them about your psychic discoveries.

The End

You and Martino both decide to take the old man up on his offer. Chico leads you along a heavily wooded path to a road behind the city hills. There is a rustic house at the end of the trail, and a van is parked in front of it. Chico goes inside the house. A few minutes later he comes back out with a man who, unfortunately, speaks no English.

"His name is Paulo," Chico tells you and Martino. "He wants you to get in the van right away. There is no time to lose."

You and Martino obey, climbing into the back of the van. Paulo jumps in and starts the engine. Chico stays behind, waving good-bye as the van pulls out onto the road and starts down a steep hill. You watch over the back of Paulo's seat as the van careens around several sharp turns.

Suddenly you see a makeshift roadblock of logs and brush up ahead. Standing behind it are several men with machine guns.

"Baixo!" Paulo yells as he jams the accelerator to the floor.

Turn to page 99.

You decide to take a chance and go with Martino. The two of you get up from the table, pay your bills, then make your way through the crowds on the sidewalk. At the corner, Martino turns down a side street and walks up to a beat-up old car.

You climb in on the passenger's side. The front seat is lumpy with broken springs, and what's left of the upholstery is stained and scratchy. Martino tries to start the car, and after several attempts it coughs into life.

Martino drives through several tunnels that are cut through the towering rock hills that divide the city into sections. Soon you reach an area where the buildings are smaller and shabbier. The stores look downright seedy compared to the sleek shops you saw in Copacabana and Ipanema.

You notice that Martino doesn't stop for red lights. In fact, he speeds up at every intersection. Fortunately, traffic is light.

"It's very dangerous to stop in these neighborhoods, particularly at red lights," he explains. "There are many thieves and robbers. That's the main reason I drive this old heap. If I parked my good car around here, it would be stripped in no time."

Go on to the next page.

Finally Martino pulls up to the curb at the base of a steep hill. You get out and follow him up a maze of narrow paths that rise steadily between buildings that are little more than shacks patched together with packing-crate lumber and cardboard. Here and there you pass a small house that is better built and stuccoed, and most of them have been painted in bright colors. Many have flower boxes in the windows. Laundry seems to be hanging everywhere.

Turn to page 104.

You reluctantly agree to wear the wire. You hate to betray Niko's trust, but it may be your only chance to find Billy and Judy. Maybe you can signal him somehow so he'll know about the wire. An unmarked police car drops you off in front of Niko's office building. His men search you before you go into his office, but they don't seem to notice the wire.

"Ah, there you are, my friend," Niko says. "But I am very disappointed. I have much information for you, but I learn that you agree to spy for police. You see I also have spies in police station."

"But I was going to signal you not to say anything incriminating," you say.

"Maybe so, but Niko can not risk chances. Very sorry that you must take shortcut thirty-three stories down to street," he says, as three of his men grab you and toss you out of one of the office windows.

The End

Many hours later, the plane lands at Narita Airport near Tokyo. When you and Judy get off the plane, you convince her to call home immediately.

"Dad isn't as upset as I thought he'd be," Judy says after hanging up the phone. She shakes her head, looking confused. "He sounded almost as if he *expected* me to go in search of Billy."

"That's a relief," you say. "Let's catch the monorail train to the city. On the way I'll point out some of the sights I remember from my last trip here."

Unfortunately, this time the approach to the city is shrouded in smog, and the tall glass skyscrapers are almost invisible. When you reach Hamamatsucho Station in downtown Tokyo, you lead Judy down into the subway.

"I know a small inn in the Asakusa district," you say. "The rooms are a cross between Western and Japanese styles. As soon as we check in, I'm going to call a special friend of mine. I still have his telephone number."

"Special? What do you mean?" Judy asks.

Turn to page 22.

You decide to take a look around the city and get your bearings. You leave the hotel and walk randomly first in one direction and then in another. In one section, you see rows of gilded temples rising high above the banks of the Chao Phraya. Another area resembles an Oriental bazaar with hundreds of brightly lit stores with colorful neon signs selling everything from electronics and clothes to toys and incense. You walk through an elegant neighborhood of large teak houses with high, winglike roofs, and then one where the people live in huts constructed of badly warped plywood and rusty sheets of tin held together by strips of tar paper.

Turn to page 97.

"You will learn soon enough. For today, just relax and enjoy the trip. There is much to see," Vajira says, handing you a pleated straw hat with a very wide brim. "Wear this when you go on deck. It will protect you from the sun and also disguise that you are an American. The Dragon may have spies watching for us along the river."

You put on your hat and go out on the platform deck at the stern. You lie down on a wicker lounge chair and watch the shore speed by. The banks are thick with vegetation except for an occasional clearing where groups of small houses of plaited bamboo are perched on stakes about six feet above the ground. Some have roofs thatched with palm leaves, and others are topped with sheets of corrugated iron. Many are surrounded by coconut palms, banana plants, and mango trees. Every once in a while you see elephants along the shore carrying huge logs.

"The elephants carry teak logs from deep in the forest down to the river for transport to Bangkok," Vajira says, joining you on the deck. "Teak is one of our major exports. Are you thirsty?"

You nod, and she hands you a glass of pinkish water. You look at it cautiously for a few seconds.

"The pink color is our way of showing that the water has been purified and is safe to drink," she says.

Turn to page 20.

A stream of sunlight coming from the entrance of the cave wakes you up. You get up groggily and walk toward it. Most of the others are still sleeping soundly, but you find Ling sitting just outside the cave. She is poring over several maps spread out on the ground.

"Good morning," she says. "I'm afraid we don't have much for breakfast—just some lotus seeds and tea. We may be able to fix something more substantial later."

Turn to page 74.

You decide to wait and see if Billy comes home on his own. If he's not back in a week or so, you'll reconsider what to do then. In the meantime, you concentrate on studying for your final exams.

One day as you are walking home from school, you notice that a car is following you. You are trying to figure out what to do when the car suddenly speeds past you and stops at the next corner.

As you approach the car, a man inside calls to you by name. You peer at him through the window and realize that he must be the dark-haired man Judy described, who visited Billy just before he disappeared.

"We need to talk," the man says. "Why don't you get in and we'll go for a little drive?"

"No thanks," you say. "If you want to talk, we can do it right here."

"All right," he says. "I am an agent of the Eagle, your friend Billy's benefactor. I have ten thousand dollars in traveler's checks for you and a plane ticket to Thailand. If you want to join your friend, you'll take the trip."

If you decide to take the mysterious man up on his offer, turn to page 108.

If you decide against it, turn to page 98.

Early the next morning, you arrive at Armada's giant cattle ranch. The bank of the river is lined with gunmen as you, Martino, and Paulo are led ashore. Armada himself, a short man with a large mustache, steps forward, pushing a dark-haired man in front of him.

"So you were looking for Senhor Barros," Armada says. "Well, here he is. And now that I have you all together, we will have a little fun."

Armada's men force you, Martino, Paulo, and Barros to the edge of the riverbank. A few feet away, the water is alive with hundreds of fish. With a sudden shock of fear, you realize that they are deadly piranha. They are darting every which way, going after pieces of meat tossed into the river by a couple of Armada's men. The rest of his men form an audience, laughing and shouting at the show. Some of them fire pistol shots at the ground near your feet, forcing you closer to the edge of the river.

Turn to page 63.

"I see you found the Capoeiras," a voice says from behind you. It's Maria, the woman from the plane.

"Oh, hello," you say. "Yes, I guess I did. I really enjoyed it."

"You did very well. Perhaps you will stay in our country and learn more of it," she says. Then she waves good-bye and vanishes into the darkness.

Turn to page 61.

You look out the window of the plane at the mountains stretching in all directions. The landscape looks ghostly in the faint moonlight. You wonder how anyone could be living down there.

"Are you sure that Billy and Judy are being held in these mountains?" you ask.

"Just before you and Vajira arrived at the base, I received a radio message from our agent in Simao, an isolated air base a hundred miles north of the Dragon's headquarters. He said that a young man and a young woman fitting your friends' descriptions were aboard one of the Dragon's planes that refueled there, then flew south."

You fly for a while longer before Ling says, "We're getting close. Watch the screen while I keep an eye on the ground."

A few minutes later, a faint point of light appears on the screen. "I see something," you say.

Ling glances at the screen. "Good. And I think I just caught a brief flash of light on the ground," she says. "Someone—perhaps a guard—could have lit a cigarette or opened a door for a second. Our location checks with the coordinates on the screen." She banks the plane sharply to the left.

Turn to page 60.

Your eyes are fixed on the ring. One of the fighters is now kneeling, the palms of his hands pressed together and placed against his forehead. The other fighter is walking around the ring, running his hand along the top rope.

"One fighter paying homage to the guardian spirit of the ring, the other sealing off the ring from evil spirits," the driver shouts close to your ear after seeing the curious look on your face. "The bands on their heads are sacred cords showing that they are Thai fighters."

The gong sounds to start the first round. The fighters rush at each other. The one in the blue trunks aims a high kick at the other's head that glances off his jaw. Almost at the same time, the fighter in the red trunks moves inside the kick and elbows his opponent hard in the chest, knocking the wind out of him. Before the fighter in the blue trunks can recover, the other fighter grabs his opponent's head between his gloves and, pulling it down, rapidly brings up both knees, one after the other, bashing him in the face. You wonder how anyone can take such punishment and stay on his feet, but the fighter in the blue trunks wrestles away, delivering several blows below the belt of the other man.

As the fight goes on, the orchestra continues to play wildly. People shout back and forth, placing bets. The drumbeats of the orchestra speed up, increasing the excitement of the crowd.

Turn to page 46.

You decide to go to the Tokyo authorities and try to explain what happened, but before you have a chance, an ambulance arrives, and you are whisked off to a hospital. You are examined by a Japanese doctor and given some pills to take. You guess that they're aspirin, but you're not sure. In any event, they help ease your headache from the crash.

After you're released from the hospital, you take the subway to the Tokyo police station. You ask for Inspector Saito or Detective Aikiko, both of whom you met on your last trip. However, both are away working on an important case. Another police officer, Inspector Toku, comes into the office. When he hears your name, he gets very excited.

"You are one that defeated my son in preliminaries of karate tournament last year. I remember," he says.

You don't know what to say. "Well . . . I mean, that was a tournament, and—" you stammer.

"Not hold it against you. You very good fighter. Even son say so. You inspire him work harder. He is grateful to you."

"I'm glad of that," you say, relieved. You explain to him about Billy and Judy.

"You also friends with Niko, head of Golden Ear Yakuza?" Toku asks you.

"Yes. I was hoping he could help me find my friend."

Turn to page 62.

Finally, you wander into a large temple. In the center of the main shrine is a gilded Buddha, thirty feet high, shining in the light of hundreds of candles at its base. You are standing there looking at it when a saffron-robed monk comes out from behind it.

"I sense a warrior who has been roaming the world looking for the ultimate principles of enlightened combat," he says.

"Not exactly," you say, "but—"

"If you enter one of our monasteries, you will learn much," he says.

"Right now I'm just looking for my friend," you reply.

"You will find your friend and much more," he says. He steps closer to you and looks into the depths of your eyes.

Turn to page 77.

"I've been told that when something sounds too good to be true, it usually is," you tell the mysterious man. "I don't know what proposition you or the Eagle sold Billy, but whatever it was, I'm not falling for it."

"Have it your way," the man says. "But don't say that I didn't offer you a good deal." He guns the engine and drives off.

Turn to page 45.

"Get down!" Martino shouts. You both flatten out on the floor. The van crashes through the barrier as a hail of bullets zing through the sides just over your head. Paulo curses as he is hit in the shoulder, but he keeps driving.

The van is soon out of town and climbing through the rolling hills to the north. Paulo stops at the side of the road so that Martino can take over the driving. You help Paulo fashion a crude bandage for his shoulder. Fortunately, his wound is not serious.

You and Paulo rest in the back while Martino drives. You doze off for a while and wake up in the cold gray light of early dawn. The coastal highway is shrouded in fog. Martino is still at the wheel. A short time later, the van turns off on a side road. After another half hour of driving, you see that the fog has lifted. You soon reach a sprawling stuccoed house basking in the bright sunlight.

Martino stops the van in front of the house. You all get out. Suddenly, with a look of fear on his face, Paulo shouts something to Martino in Portuguese.

Turn to page 52.

"I can't leave Japan without finding Judy first," you tell Niko. "Just give me a clue as to where this Dragon guy might be holding her."

Niko laughs. "You are fearless fighter. Even my own men shake when Dragon is mentioned. Dragon's men are everywhere and nowhere— like ninjas. I have only one address that is possibility. It is a warehouse in Yokohama."

The next morning, you take a high-speed train to Yokohama, and after some searching around the waterfront, you locate the warehouse.

That night, you return to the warehouse and approach it very cautiously, moving slowly through the shadows behind the building. It seems deserted. But unseen by you, one of the Dragon's guards is watching silently in the darkness as you start to climb up the side of the warehouse toward a window high above. He finishes you off from behind with a silent arrow from a *yumi*, the small but powerful bow carried by the ninjas.

The End

"I'm very sorry, but I just can't do that to a friend," you say.

"Very well, then. Your passport for Japan now invalid. One of officers will escort you to airport for next available flight to your country," the inspector says.

"Hey, wait a minute," you say. "That's not fair. My friends are missing and—"

"Very sorry, but is way it is." Toku motions for his assistant to take you away. "We will notify you when we find them. Bye-bye."

You try to argue further, but it's no use. As your plane back to the United States takes off, you stare out the window, hoping the Tokyo police will be able to find your friends.

The End

Suddenly, your feet slip off. You hang on desperately, struggling to find the bottom rope again.

Your hands on the top rope are half frozen in the cold, and you don't know how much longer you can hold on. You thrash around desperately with your legs. Then your feet find the bottom rope, just in time.

Finally, you make it across. You collapse on the ground, shaking with fright.

Ling comes across last. "Come on, we must hurry," she says.

You pull yourself together and get to your feet. After another hour of hiking through the mountains, you reach a spot just below the Dragon's headquarters.

"This is the most dangerous part," Ling whispers. You follow her as she creeps toward the base of the huge stone fortress above.

Turn to page 69.

When you are almost to the top of the hill, Martino stops in front of one of the better-built homes. He steps up onto the small front porch and knocks on the door.

You glance back down the steep hill you've just climbed. The people who live here may be poor, but they certainly have a spectacular view. Necklaces of light curve around the darkened beaches, and the huge, illuminated statue with outstretched arms seems to float high above the scene on top of Corcovado Mountain.

A dark-skinned, white-haired old man appears at the door of the house.

"We have come to see your son," Martino says.

"He was here, but he left over an hour ago," the old man replies.

"Do you know where he went?" Martino asks him.

"I could not tell you even if I knew. Armada's assassins are after him."

"I'm not surprised," Martino says. "Your son has become a thorn in Armada's side."

"Who is this Armada? And why would he want to kill Senhor Barros?" you ask.

Go on to the next page.

"José Armada is a very powerful man," the old man tells you. "He owns the largest ranch in the Amazon, and he has been illegally burning thousands of acres of virgin forest to increase the size of his grazing lands. My son has been trying to stop him—he has written letters of protest to everyone in the government. And it's having an effect. The National Congress is considering cracking down on Armada despite his many paid supporters."

Turn to page 19.

You decide to see something of the city. You wander down the road that runs along the beach. Down by the water, you see a string of flickering lights. Many people are heading in that direction, and you follow, curious about where they're going.

When you reach the edge of the sea, you find that long rows of burning candles have been stuck in the sand. Behind the candles are groups of figures dressed in white with necklaces of flowers. They are twirling around in a kind of trance.

Farther down the beach, two figures are engaged in a dancelike mock combat to the accompaniment of a drum and a strange-looking one-stringed instrument shaped like an archer's bow.

You walk closer, fascinated, as they move their legs with sweeping movements, striking high into the air, all to the rhythm of the drumbeat. The movements remind you of the tae kwon do you learned in Korea.

Suddenly, a foot is zooming directly toward your chin. You swerve to one side as it barely misses and counter with a karate kick of your own, careful to keep to the rhythm of the dance. You find yourself moving around with them, getting into the spirit of their technique.

After a while, the music stops. The crowd that has formed around you applauds. *"Muito Bem!"* one of the dancers exclaims, patting you on the back before running off down the beach.

Turn to page 92.

"All right, I'll go," you say. "What do I do next?"

"The checks are in this envelope. Just sign them and they're yours. There's a first-class plane ticket in there, too. Your flight leaves tomorrow afternoon."

The man hands you an envelope, guns his motor, and speeds away. You pull out the checks and the ticket and examine them carefully. They look genuine.

You go home and tell your parents about the mysterious stranger's offer.

"You find that man right away and give the tickets and money back," your mother says firmly.

"But this could be my money for college," you argue. "And it doesn't look as if Billy's coming back on his own. I *should* try to find him."

It takes a lot more wheedling on your part, but finally your parents reluctantly agree to let you go. The next afternoon, your father drives you to the airport.

Eighteen hours later, your plane lands in Bangkok, the capital of Thailand. You check into one of the finest hotels in the city. You are eager to start looking for Billy right away.

Turn to page 85.

You decide to go back to your hotel. After all, you really don't have any information that Armada would want. You say good-bye to Martino and the others and walk down to the main street. You hail a cab, and when you get in you give the driver the address of your hotel. The taxi pulls away from the curb and speeds in the opposite direction from Copacabana. You lean forward and give the driver the address again, but he doesn't seem to understand.

The driver keeps looking back at you nervously. You suddenly realize that something is terribly wrong. You are trying to decide what to do when the cab screeches to a halt. The driver leaps out and starts running toward the beach. You open the rear door and start to get out, but it's too late. The cab erupts into a gigantic fireball.

The End

When the waiter comes back with your food, you ask him about Senhor Barros.

"Senhor Barros? I haven't seen him tonight. That is unusual. He's almost always here about this time," the waiter replies. He promises to let you know if Barros shows up.

The meal is delicious. You finish eating quickly, and you are about to ask again about Barros when a dark-haired man with a small mustache comes over from the next table and sits opposite you.

"My name is Martino Campos. I am a journalist working for *Manchete*. You've heard of it?"

"As a matter of fact, I have," you say.

Turn to page 56.

112

You know you've reached Brazil when the pilot announces that you're about to fly over the Amazon River. The plane descends to a lower altitude so that the passengers can get a better look. You look down at the wide river twisting through the jungle in a seemingly endless series of curves. The jungle stretches in every direction to the horizon.

The plane climbs back to its cruising altitude. A few hours later it begins its approach to Rio's international airport. Maria leans over and points out the sights to you.

"That's Corcovado Peak off to the right, the one with the giant statue on top. And the bay that we're approaching is called Guanabara."

As the plane glides smoothly in for a landing, you thank Maria for her help and say good-bye. Then you take the airport bus to the Meridien-Rio, the hotel that Maria recommended.

You check into the hotel and get a room on the twenty-sixth floor. It has a panoramic view of the beach on the other side of a broad boulevard and the ocean beyond. In the distance several colorful hang gliders drift down from the sky, seemingly in slow motion.

Turn to page 39.

You decide to take the more direct route across the rope bridge. When the rest of the group is awake and ready, Ling divides everyone into two teams. When darkness falls, you set off with Ling and several of her best fighters. An hour later, you reach the bridge. The others start across, disappearing one by one into the darkness. You can't see the chasm below, but you know from Ling's description that it must be incredibly deep. Soon it's your turn to cross.

As you grab the rope, you think you hear a muffled scream in front of you. You hope it's just the wind and not somebody falling off the bridge. You inch forward, carefully sliding your feet along the bottom rope.

Turn to page 102.

You decide to stay behind and maintain radio contact with the plane. Ling and Vajira climb in and take off.

A few minutes later the radio crackles in front of you. "Can you read me?" you say into the microphone.

"Yes, I read you loud and clear," Ling replies.

As the hours go by, however, the signal gets weaker and weaker. Also, you begin to hear sounds of movement outside the radio shack. It's just the wind, you figure. But finally your curiosity gets the better of you, and you cautiously look outside.

There is a whir in the air. You try to duck, but it's too late. One of the famous curved Thai throwing knives finds its target in your chest.

The End

ABOUT THE AUTHOR

RICHARD BRIGHTFIELD is a graduate of Johns Hopkins University, where he studied biology, psychology, and archaeology. For many years he worked as a graphic designer at Columbia University. He has written many books in the Choose Your Own Adventure series, including *Master of Kung Fu, Master of Tae Kwon Do, Hijacked!,* and *Master of Karate.* In addition, Mr. Brightfield is the author of *The Valley of the Kings* and *South of the Border,* the first two books in The Young Indiana Jones Chronicles series. He has coauthored more than a dozen game books with his wife, Glory. The Brightfields and their daughter, Savitri, now live on the coast of southern Florida.

ABOUT THE ILLUSTRATOR

FRANK BOLLE studied at Pratt Institute. He has worked as an illustrator for many national magazines and now creates and draws cartoons for magazines as well. He has also worked in advertising and children's educational materials and has drawn and collaborated on several newspaper comic strips, including *Annie* and *Winnie Winkle.* He has illustrated many books in the Choose Your Own Adventure series, most recently *The Lost Ninja, Daredevil Park, Kidnapped!, The Terrorist Trap, Ghost Train,* and *Magic Master.* He is also the illustrator of *The Valley of the Kings* and *South of the Border,* the first two books in The Young Indiana Jones Chronicles series. A native of Brooklyn Heights, New York, Mr. Bolle now lives and works in Westport, Connecticut.

CHOOSE YOUR OWN ADVENTURE®

Bantam Books, Dept. AV6, 2451 South Wolf Road, Des Plaines, IL 60018

Please send me the items I have checked above. I am enclosing $_____
(please add $2.50 to cover postage and handling). Send check or money order,
no cash or C.O.D.s please.

Mr/Ms _____

Address _____

City/State _____ Zip _____

AV6-4/92

Please allow four to six weeks for delivery.
Prices and availability subject to change without notice.

A CHOOSE YOUR OWN ADVENTURE® BOOK

PASSPORT

THE NEWS TEAM THAT COVERS THE WORLD

YOU MAKE THE NEWS!

You are an anchor for the Passport news team.
Together with Jake, your cameraman, and Eddy,
an investigative journalist, you travel the world on
assignment, covering firsthand some of the hottest
events in the news.

JOIN THE

The exciting series from the creator of *CHOOSE YOUR OWN ADVENTURE*®

Join the universe's most elite group of galactic fighters as you make your moves in this interactive series—
SPACE HAWKS!
Meet your fellow space travellers and become a part of the faster-than-light action.

Each **SPACE HAWKS** adventure is illustrated by comic book artist Dave Cockrum!